DOGS
IN
DISGUISE

In memory of my mum, who loved dogs
(especially small, daft dachshunds)

P.B.

For Jessica and Hannah

J.B.

First published in hardback by HarperCollins *Children's Books* in 2021
First published in paperback in 2022

HarperCollins *Children's Books* is a division of HarperCollins*Publishers* Ltd
1 London Bridge Street, London SE1 9GF

www.harpercollins.co.uk

HarperCollins*Publishers*
1st Floor, Watermarque Building, Ringsend Road, Dublin 4, Ireland

1 3 5 7 9 10 8 6 4 2

Text copyright © Peter Bently 2021
Illustrations copyright © John Bond 2021

ISBN: 978-0-00-846917-7

Printed in Italy

DOGS
IN
DISGUISE

BY PETER BENTLY
& JOHN BOND

HarperCollins *Children's Books*

DOGS come in all kinds of
COLOURS and SIZES,

BUT when **no one's** looking
they put on **DISGUISES.**

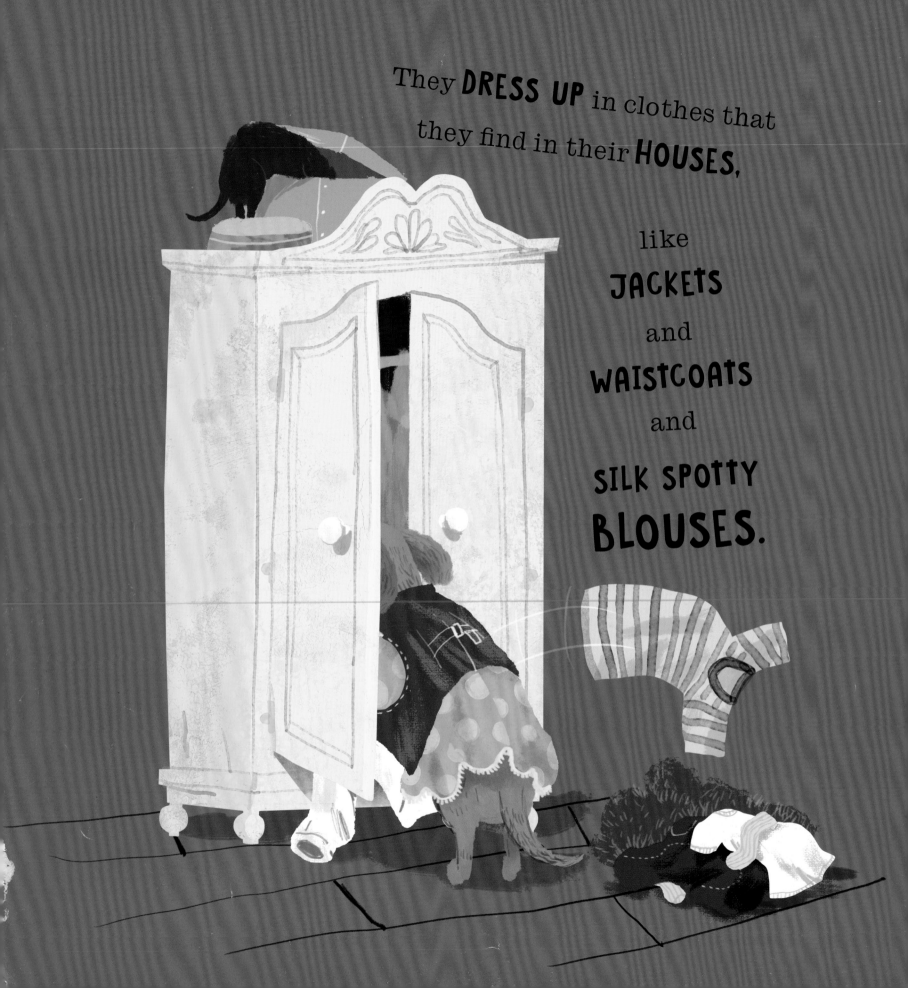

They **DRESS UP** in clothes that they find in their **HOUSES,**

like **JACKETS** and **WAISTCOATS** and **SILK SPOTTY BLOUSES.**

HATS and **HIGH HEELS** help to make them look big –

and sometimes they'll stick on a **BEARD** or a **WIG.**

POOCHES love mooching about at the store,

where **NO DOGS ALLOWED** is the sign on the door.

But who's in that **SWEATER?**
It's Sadie the **SETTER.**

PAY
HERE

And there, in
PINK TROUSERS?

A pair of **OLD SCHNAUZERS.**

It's **STRICTLY NO DOGS**

at the Café Celeste,

and you aren't

allowed in if

you're

not smartly

dressed –

like this

elegant gent

in the

TRENCHCOAT

and **HAT**.

It's a family of **FRENCHIES!**

Well, just fancy that!

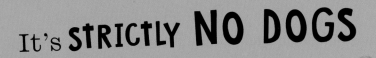

PEREGRINE PUG,
in **TUXEDO** and **'TASH,**
is already there
scoffing sausage
and mash.

For **DOGS** who like sport,
there's a very tough rule:
ALL DOGS are **BANNED** in the
gym and the pool.

BUT no one spots **SPIKE** having fun with the woggles,
DISGUISED in his bright orange **SWIMSUIT** and **GOGGLES**.

And the folk in the gym cheer
the champ at **JUJITSU** –

if only they
knew it was
CHARLENE the
SHIH-TZU!

The **DOGS** all start early to learn **DRESSING-UP**.

The grown-up DOGS teach
it to every young PUP.

Sometimes the youngsters aren't terribly wise
and forget that they're meant to be
dressed in **DISGUISE.**

"GNUS?" laughed the keeper. "You're pulling my leg.

Gnus don't chase squirrels — or SIT UP and BEG!"

And when folks had a barbecue down at the park,
BARNEY THE BEAGLE went too, for a lark.

He thought he'd

sneak in as a

very small tree

and snaffle a

nice tasty

BURGER or **THREE.**

Poor **BARNEY.**

He ended up feeling a fool

because he'd forgotten a

VERY BIG rule:

Of all **DOG DISGUISES,**

a tree is the **WORST . . .**

Unless you tell **ALL** of the other dogs **FIRST!**

But most
DOG DISGUISES
are cunning
and smart.

They're stunningly skilful at looking the part.

So the next time you're somewhere
that **DOGS** are **FORBIDDEN**,
there are sure to be **POOCHES**,
all cleverly hidden.

Those soldiers lined up on parade in the sun?
Look a bit closer. They're **DOGS**, every one!

And who's **MUNCHING** snacks at the matinee show?

It's those **FRENCHIES** again, sitting all in a row!

And it's not just on Earth that
the **DOGS** wear **DISGUISE** –

just take a look

way up there in the skies.

Who's in the rocket ship off to the **STARS?**

It's the
COCKAPOO
COSMONAUTS,

heading for
MARS!